CAPITAL LOVE

CAPITAL LOVE:

A LOVE CELEBRATION FROM
WASHINGTON WRITERS' PUBLISHING HOUSE

EDITED BY CAROLINE BOCK AND JONA COLSON

Washington Writers' Publishing House
Washington, D.C.

FIRST EDITION

COVER DESIGN by Dave Ring
TYPOGRAPHY by Barbara Shaw

ISBN 978-1-941551-54-7

Library of Congress Control Number: 2026938682

Printed in the United States of America

WASHINGTON WRITERS' PUBLISHING HOUSE
2814 5th Street, NE, #1301
Washington, D.C. 20017
More information: www.washingtonwriters.org

Support for Washington Writers' Publishing House comes from the DC Commission on Arts & Humanities, the Maryland State Arts Council, and the Community of Literary Magazines & Presses

To all those who believe love is the antidote to hate,
and that love is action, intent, healing, and hope,
Capital Love is for you.

TABLE OF CONTENTS

"When love is present the desire to dominate and exercise power cannot rule the day..."

– bell hooks in *All About Love*

KYLE G. DARGAN

NEVER BOTHER MAKING LOVE IN A LINCOLN BEDROOM

Back in the pandemic's throes, there was a government scientist
who would summon me to Upper Marlboro to ignite me like sage – the smoke
from her striking and my smouldering a veiled measure to purge
divorce's remnant from that mansion and her body's conduits.
There was no outside then. (Remember?) The two of us scattered
ash about all that square footage. We did it in the basement bathroom,
the empty family room, around the mudroom's gauntlet of shoes,
the master shower. We featured in the defunct home theatre, pressed
prone in the meditation room, bounced before the audience of framed degrees
and plaques in her study. The bed rendered superfluous, but there too.

When the capital decided it was bored with caution, and we all
crept back to offices and the stress of being the free world's
supposed nerve center, she snuffed me and tucked away her flame.
Maybe we had scented those rooms, but that house remained an armory
of anxieties. I knew she worked for Defense, but too there was war within her
I had no hope of ceasing. *You don't come here and change Washington.*
You come here and Washington changes you. Eight years of Obama
should have taught me that. I had consulted for the White House,
addressed the Library of Congress, but never had I been fully on the inside –
not until her twining my heart, drawing me deeper into the State.

SAMANTHA NEUGEBAUER

LIVES LIGHTER THAN OUR OWN

We lived in the age of accountability and we were all amateur accountants, compiling the lightness and heaviness of lives. Even after our work bored us, it left its residue on our minds, like fingerprints on glass, and everyone was glass.

We waited for normal to come again. But normal was 1997, and the listification and commercialization of our nostalgia was ruining our nostalgia, anyway, and our past alongside it too, cataracting our memories with greasy presentisms and adult anxieties.

> Under the Nazi regime, Benjamin wrote "The Work of Art in the Age of Mechanical Reproduction," prognosing how reproduction would devalue the aura (uniqueness) of a work of art. Now it is ourselves we reproduce, and it is our own auras we feel diminishing.

We attempt to rearrange the deck chairs on the Titanic while rewatching *Titanic* in 3D, and afterward, on Instagram, Kate Winslet saying *nepotism isn't real* at her son's movie premiere.

> Only our disappointment is real.
> We were promised the moon and the stars.

We know it's wrong to be an *I*. *I* belongs to the boom boom's, our parents' generation. Yet we can't quite kick them, or the *I*, off completely. Instead, we land somewhere in the middle, localizing our *I* in small groups, a kind of compromise with ourselves.

Actually, America already had the moon when we were born.

But we don't deserve it anymore, and maybe *we* never did—that's the worst part: what we've loved is faulty and loving too much, even now, makes us bad accountants.

VICTORIA SOSA

STELLAR EVOLUTION

Baby, it's basic physics. Greatness is amassed.
The bigger your influence, the more you attract with your blue luminous beauty.

Baby, you're the hottest thing to ever bless these weaker beings
with a blinding light that burns like love, hurts like love,
takes and takes and aches like love.

Baby don't whine, "my life is a mess"
when you're red-hot iron, when you're white-hot sex.
So you're feeling out of balance, add a little more excess.
Hopelessness is power, collapse under the stress.

Baby, real greatness is a singleness of focus.
There's a horizon between your thighs.
A line-of-no-return.
Let them dive into your darkness,
be ripped apart for words.

ALEX CARRIGAN

SMALL SPARKS

Should we kiss in front of the National Guard?
Should we add some passion to this metro station?

We could easily add some passion to this metro station
with just a giggle and a quick peck on the lips,

but would just a giggle and a quick peck on the lips
make those masked men reach for their service weapons?

Would they draw their service weapons and bark
because of your race or because of our gender?

Lately, because of your race and our gender,
we don't hold each other's hands on the streets.

We can't hold hands on these streets anymore
in case we hear the jackboots stomp towards us.

But in case the jackboots do stomp towards us,
should we kiss in front of the National Guard?

CHANLEE LUU

ON A TREE STUMP, SARASOTA

Everybody thinks the succulent
flesh of rambutan is the treasure.

The furry skin and seed discarded
after the fruit is mawed.

The world always favors the sweet–
They can't handle the tough, the unsightly,

The red, the hidden, the anchors
Of all things beautiful.

That's us. You, covering me
On my worst days. I, the seed,

that grows or vice
versa–the cycle
never ending.

THERESE DOUCET

THE POMEGRANATE

Under Persephone's gaze, its skin appears rough, like the dark, still-quivering organs the soothsayers read as omens: A hard, round heart. It sits on the ebony slab as though forgotten, next to it a slim silver knife and a painted glazed bowl to catch the seeds. Inside, she knows, is a labyrinth. You slice off its crown, make shallow incisions through the leathery surface. The arils cluster in waves around a maze of bitter white membranes, twisting and turning like the cave tunnels Hades led her down when he carried her to this place. No straight paths without or within. A deep cut into the pomegranate wastes the juices. The proper way is to extract the burstable arils inside gently, peel off a little skin at a time, follow the folds and hills and valleys within, stroke them with a fingertip so they fall as though of their own accord, lift each patch of veil as it is denuded of its treasure.

Hades comes to stand by her, head bowed, eyes lowered, seeming ashamed now of the fierce passion that led him to her violent capture. *Are you hungry?* he asks. She tries to meet his eyes and sees it is he who is full of hunger. They both look away quickly. *Yes*, she says. He takes up the knife, begins to cut the pomegranate, delicately, painstakingly. He does it correctly, until six seeds gleam on the cold stone table's surface. He's learning, she thinks. She eats them one by one.

BRANDON BLUE

A ROOM OF ONE'S OWN OR ORGY IN WHICH EVERYONE IS BLACK

Here each person undresses
to accommodate the other
to become the darkness between
our bodies, to pull each other close.

We strip the arguments of our lives
into plastic bags to sublime
into a room that no other room can hold:
a vase holding few Bearded Irises tangle,

the petals thumb the lip for stability, hanging
counter balance on what they can depend; brother to brother—
At an angle, with a porno projected on the wall,
you might see a shadow stroking me, gently, but it is me

whispering to myself: this space is supple and brief.
And when we must leave, we depose to jeans and bodies, again.

JONA COLSON

GOOD GRACE

I didn't pray enough. Left
church too early, and no Sunday

school or summer study.
It's personal, isn't it,

when you try to pull all these lies
out of my hands—

and some kind of truth, even
if it doesn't breathe like a fish

in the good water of grace?

GRACE CAVALIERI

AT 94, NOT THE BURLESQUE YOU MAKE IT TO BE

You may think there's none left, a life doubled in length and clarity—
You imagine the emotional withholding, the slunk-wilted lilies
    a painful revelation of roses,
You see Age as adroit with lost appetite, a saddened clump of history—
Surprisingly, the past's burlap scenes can be warm satin with their wrapping—
    'tho clouds may lose suites of stars,
And I admit there's more precision in the sloppiness and splendor of Love—
Profusions of images made The Former Time splendid, every nativity a statement
    flights are remembered, agile and eager,
Yet! You'd be surprised, in leaning back and coiled within, wildcats are ready to sprin

TAMAR SHAPIRO

TRUTH OR LOVE

Do you have parents? my mother asks. We are in the kitchen, yellow light on wooden floors, paned glass, wintery black outside. We are pretending my mother baked the root vegetables that fill the kitchen with sweet, earthy regret. She turns toward me with her lost eyes, her unwashed hair, and sees me, fifty years old, wilting chin, crevassed neck, black boots, black sweater, tight black jeans.

All that black and still not youthful.

We walked together that morning, stooping to clutch a leaf, raising its veined translucence to the ice-grey air, and she asked the same question. *Do you have parents?* I hugged her sideways, felt her frail bones vanish within my arms like her memory. *I am your daughter,* I said. But it was wrong. All wrong. My mother shrank from me, new lines cutting her already lined face.

Why do you tell me these strange stories? Stop telling me these strange stories.

The kitchen table stands between us now, vegetables in a bowl, burnt edges on orange. *Do you have parents?* my mother repeats. My own motherhood has not prepared me for this. Bruised childbirth, midnight teeth sucking at me, skin hanging over the scar of two c-sections. My body is a settling foundation. My mother has grown tiny again, bird-like. I touch the raised spots on her hand, calm her nervous fingers.

No, I say. *I do not have parents.*
Why not? my mother asks. *Are they dead?*
Yes, I say. *Yes, they are dead.*

CHRIS BILES

THE STRENGTH OF SOFTNESS

every fist has a softness at its core
opening is the key – our palms

placed to face the palms of others
gentle touch, interlocking fingers

free feelings other than fear
other than hate, gentle touch

and the power in its reminder
can melt what's frozen, can melt

the ice when we stubbornly clutch
the shards shoved in our faces

frozen blades become warm water
in our grasp – strong, soft – warm

water to cleanse the cuts, to wash
the inevitable, to help its healing

CHRIS BILES

WHAT LADY LIBERTY ASKS US TO HOLD

(Inspired by the protest poster)

Girl, hold my earrings. Hold my bag, hold my jacket, hold my gloves so these punches really hurt. Let them come at this scrappy Lady, I am tenacious in the face of their brazen belligerence. Rage in my temples, blood pulsing, heart bursting in hatred – theirs, mine. Yet, strangely, at the same time, the body feels so hollow when filled with fear. Blood blooming in an empty vessel. I am frightened. I don't know when I'll reach my limit, when I'll break. I need to stop – if just to breathe, to catch my breath, catch the fact that I somehow went not only to a state of *fight* but also to one of *flight*, and with my feet crafted to stand on broken shackles, symbol of freedom, that's not something I'm meant to consider.

Girl, drop my earrings. Drop my bag, jacket, gloves, and all the rest and just hold my hand. Girl, hold my hand so it stops trembling. Hold my hand so the softness of your palm shows me the other side of this fight. Girl, show me the necessary balance, what we're fighting for, why I stand on these broken chains: it's the dream of love – a dead love now, but one that can be resurrected; a love we're mourning, but a love when mourned will take us forward, will take us into tomorrow, and maybe tomorrow will at long last be a new day rather than the maddening repetition of history.

Girl, hold my hand.

CHARLOTTE VAN SCHAACK

THE FIRST TIME I WAS CALLED A SLUR WAS THE DAY I REALIZED WHAT LOVE WAS

I had never considered that love also meant trust. I was independent, self-reliant. I did dumb things like swimming in my clothes when my friends and I spent the day in a river to escape humidity so dense that breathing would have been easier with gills. Of course, it rained on us. We got soaked, crawled out over rocks, and spread ourselves out to dry on picnic tables under a wooden shelter. At the far end, some teens huffed and gawked at us.

"We're not sharing our spot with some queers," barely audible as they abandoned the space.

I wasn't in love with any of my friends, but I thought I could be. And what scared me was that these kids did too. I didn't know I was queer yet. No one had stopped me to make me wonder why I didn't care about love. My best friends and I were all as disappointingly unobjectifiable as teenage girls could come, and at seventeen, it wouldn't be long until some of us realized we weren't girls either.

Nothing happened that day, but one of my friends was given a knife by her mom's boyfriend when she recounted the story. I remember feeling lacerations in my lungs, the air cut of humidity and sharpened by the storm. In that moment, I didn't know what to do besides give up, give myself over to someone else to know what to do. Eventually, I realized they always would.

ELLEN ARONOFSKY COLE

TINY GLOBE

who knew an old woman like me
had so many marbles to lose

each a miniature earth   an eddy of green & blue

when I was a child I carried constellations in my pocket

so often now I dither and you   dearest   muddle too—
our marbles commingling

I strip off my dress and stretch out beside you
just skin-on-skin a kiss landed   a caress

we could even be lounging on Aegean shores
a God and Goddess made of perilous flesh

the sea a waver of opal and birds

in a scatter of dust   I find one of yours—an aggie
                I hold it in my palm for a moment

how lovely the tiny globe looks in the late sun

S. SHAW

TO THE HEAVENS

Yo mama has one
Arm, she swims in a circle
Gathering up folks
Tossed to the edges of life
Raven-black edges snatched to God

CHRISTINA DAUB

MOURNING DOVES

Some days when January's drifts block
the door and ice swords bar my windows,
when it's hard to remember the hearth's cold
ashes were once fire, and I want to give up
on the world, on what it's become,
love enters in the swoop-and-three-waves
of dove song—the black cat pawing
the glass because huddled a few feet away,
two doves, unruffled in icy wind, grip
a thin branch and rest. Whether in their cells
or in the fusion of their bones, they know
that ice must melt, this shadowed snow—
what winter locks in eventually must grow.

HOLLY KARAPETKOVA

GRATITUDE

For an hour the rain lashed the cabin
roof, thunder shredding the sky until
we could not hear one another speak,
our anger with each other left
to simmer, danger drawing us
together in the small bed.
Then suddenly it stopped;
I could hear your breath rising
in relief and the same silence
that had seemed so caustic
before the storm now settled
over us like a gift, our gratitude
for a world that could hold
that much rage and let us live.

KAETOCHI NWODO

MARCH 27

This morning my wife's eyes are storm clouds. I have never seen them this dark. Perhaps she is reflecting my inner squall, saying *ihunanya*, I see you. Her lips twitch when she looks at me, heartbreaking tenderness wrapping an involuntary smile. Her skin is soft and her arms are strong as she holds me and tells me that she is not going anywhere; that she misses her too.

The day broke hours ago but I did not go to the dock this morning. I do not see the sunburst. I do not hear the avian hymn. I do not speak to my daughter. Instead, I seek evil as I shelter in a planetary cataclysm, watching the human species battle extinction.

I ignore paradise and watch horrors on screen because I am trying to survive my own unseen horrors. My comforter clings to me as she slides back into slumber. Renee's arms are around me, and her stormy eyes are closed, and I watch people die because I cannot look at my own beautiful world. Perhaps I can face the sun and the birds and my ghost after I have witnessed the destruction of another Earth.

BARBARA WESTWOOD DIEHL

WE CAN TIP BIG, OR

we can tell the cashier, who has to ask every single person in the line at Panera Bread if they're a rewards member, and we say *No, do you offer an AARP discount?*—which they don't—and the cashier says *Sorry* like we're the second-grade teacher whose Bic pen she stole but still made sure there was at least one Valentine in her crumpled brown paper bag with crayon hearts on it—and the cashier says she would give an AARP discount if she could and looks at us like her heart is breaking

—we can tell this cashier that her eyeliner is fabulous—that cat's eye style—and her Lauren Bacall voice is magical, and we can give her the Maybelline coupon from our purse because, we tell her, for us, *It'd be like putting lipstick on a pig* (though we still like Great Lash mascara).

We can tip big—but if we can't tip big—when the Department of Public Works guy in the yellow vest and coveralls behind us grumbles while we count out ones and pennies, we can recommend the beef chili because with that *muscular physique* he needs protein, which makes his cheeks turn red and the cashier giggle and the ice break between the DPW guy and the cashier and me like snow before the V-blade on the Snowdogg plow parked outside. We *can* tip big, hear me. We can.

SUSAN SCHEID

PERSONAL AD

Single raindrop
seeking other raindrops
for a storm.
Let's shower this world
with kindness.
No lightning or thunder
need apply.

LAURA SHOVAN

TWISTER

My voice stretches upstairs,
asking if you've fed the dog.

You hop over a pile of dirty clothes.
I slip outside to pull the weeds.

We're always in motion. You're baking fish
while I sweep the kitchen tiles.

How did we get so twisted, pretzeled
out of shape by daily tasks?

You step around me to open the refrigerator.
I roll away when we say goodnight.

But in sleep, your heel touches my shin.
I thread a hand under your arm.

The scar on your spine brushes my navel.
My mouth unravels against your ear.

MAURA WAY

ENDURANCE 1985

The fitness test told us that
the flexed-arm hang could
make us all award-winning
girls, according to presidential
standards. Kari could stay up
there all day, and she beat the
boys at pull-ups too. There we
were, just down the road from
the White House, but Mr. Moss
never did award those patches.
I doubt our P.E. teachers ever
filled out all that paperwork,
and who could blame them? In the end,
we didn't need Ronald Reagan
to tell us who to look up to.

OLIVIA BRALEY

ICE

January 27, 2026

The newspaper owned by one of the richest men in human history runs a headline: *"Extreme Cold Spell Shaping Up as DC's Longest in 150 Years."* On the third day, I decide to free my car. The ice is so white & solid it is like breaking plates. It even makes that same noise. Last week I protested ICE three times, before & after their latest murder. At one, the brittle wood of my picket sign tears a hole in the thumb of my glove. At another, we chant in Spanish: *El pueblo unido jamás será vencido* & *Chinga la migra*. We are in the heart of the Capital, the belly of the beast. There are security cameras everywhere. I break up the ice on my car until the sharp plastic edge of my tool splinters. Frozen, I feel an outsized wave of defeat. *The world is so cold I don't know what to do,* I think, knowing the metaphor is heavy-handed. But I, too, am handling heaviness lately: grief, yes, & also armfuls of groceries, a 9-month-old exceeding all growth benchmarks. My neighbor approaches with a shovel in one hand & a hammer in the other. He passes me the former. Two hours later, my car is out. I thank him, say before he came out, I didn't know what to do. *I just figure, we're a community or whatever,* he says. *Yes*. Tomorrow there is a vigil. There will be hundreds of us clutching small flames in the cold. All we have is each other. I think that is enough.

TAMIA WILLIAMS

MARCHING ALONG THE NATIONAL MALL

Even under ice
Cherry blossom roots remain
To flare bright with spring.

ALFONSO "SITO" SASIETA

TANKA

For fear of being
tossed, we write dogma in lead
gray-dead syllables,
forgetting love undulates
& sways, our protest signs raised.

CAROLINE BOCK

DEAR AMERICA

I don't know when I stopped loving you—it was before you tore down that city on a hill; it was after Pop died—it would have broken him—he volunteered for you and was proudest that he served in one of the first desegregated infantry fighting units in Korea. Said he hit the number when his mother chose the Bronx instead of Warsaw. When her two older, curly-haired sisters—they were all dressmakers in Paris—slipped back home to care for their dying mother, and my grandmother, Rose, sailed on to a short-tempered Russian, it was truly for you; a freethinker, she came for you. Soon, letters from Warsaw begged for safe passage too. You said no. The sisters perished in the ghetto of cholera, or dysentery, or starvation; sometimes the two traverse my dreams like Chagall's flying women, and I wake weeping. In the past, I've dismissed your missteps and lies. Sometimes lovers go astray. You had ideals. You had that damn city on the hill. I should have slept with others, sought their comforts and citizenship. Yet all those things I loved about you—Beat poetry, jazz, downtowns, a swaggering of civil debate and dissent, and wide-open spaces with room enough for many more—I must lay bare, I still love. It's breaking me: You've become an ugly-talking, jabbering old man; you've lost all those sexy ideals of democracy, but I still want you, need you. Make me love you again, America, dear America.

JOSH MAHLER

AUBREY

Having the lake to return to is of the small pleasures
in my life. I watch as my sister dips my niece
into the water, the laughter as hope that the music
of family reminds me of my cousins and I standing on
the edge, casting our lines into the swirling surface
for no reason, just being there among the bugs and trees,
the fish darting away from engines and the simple
movements of the earth. Let me remember the scene
like a photograph: my sister holding her close,
as little hands hold the dancing light of the setting sun.

KEITH DAVID PARSONS

KNOW HER

Behold a modern mystery: mysticetus sporting a hundred-year harpoon in her hide like an
Overlarge nose-piercing from the eighteen-nineties. Grimacing. Barnacled.
Wanderer of northern wastes; largest mouth in creation raised. Raking seas for sustenance.
Heart singing. Surveillance of orcas, orgies, blessed brief breedings. Cetacean stories.
Ever she. Knows the strings, longings, of voluptuous life under ice. Being. Birthed.
Antebellum, ere Ishmael was conceived by Melville. Erudite. Does she judge now, this nation?
Did she oppose slavery; support suffrage? We know only her wound.

JASON GEBHARDT

DESCRIPTION OF A LOVE SONNET

Of all the love sonnets I've written
the whole *Arabian Nights* of them
the one thousand and second is unspeakable
having finally captured the shimmering blue
of the peacock's feathers   the true tenderness
of an infant's grip   my heart's entire holdings
so perfect   it has no use for end rhyme
or pentameter   I'd be summarily executed
merely for reciting it   but that's O.K.
when I listen close on the quietest nights   silence
broken by a car's passing   the branch scrape
against the window   breath   these shadow lines
that you are permitted to hear   will suffice
to say   I have loved all that could be

EMILY BLUMBERG

THE STORYTELLER

Every so often, she tells herself the story once more: a recitation usually reserved for vows or performances or grand, televised speeches. As long as we both shall live, the show will begin momentarily. I have a dream. There was a for rent sign in the window. The sun shone on her face that morning. Four girls, on the precipice of women, hugged in a circle in the creaky, barren living room. She walks the four blocks to the most beautiful building she has ever seen as often as she can: a shining, commanding dome sparkling in a delightfully empty blue sky. A castle on a hill, seemingly impenetrable, overlooking its kingdom of light with doting eyes. How strange to fall in love with something as you are told it is no longer yours. A sense of desperation in the increasingly clouded air, retreating into the small world of yourself, because where else is there to go. It is impossible, she thinks, to walk through this place without wincing, as these small, pocketed problems escape onto the brick-laid sidewalk. It is impossible, our time is over, this city will never be the same. And yet. Our laughter echoes down the street, traveling west on East Capitol, no use for a compass now. A stroke of luck, one after the other, holding beloved, historic architecture on stilts to keep the flood at bay. The world sitting still, waiting, as she lives to tell the tale, falling in love all over again.

SID GOLD

NOT QUITE LOVE POEM #8

Those days
you feel so cut
& chewed
by the world
nothing remains
but gristle & bone

Is the long-gone sound
of my voice
all it would take
to make you whole?

KIRSTEN SHU-YING CHEN

ODE TO THE LOCAL NEWS

Everyone's always saying *how are you*
When we could be asking *what's got your attention*?
The day is a slaughterhouse
but the mind is a prayer factory
and I don't understand not wanting
to get to the point.
Today there was an earthquake!
Yesterday they shut down F&C bagel
and the card store too.
It can be hard to come to terms
with our own powerlessness—
but you know, for us, these are the days.
So may they begin with thanks
and may they end in survival
even when the whole world breaks beneath you
taking all you've known and loved
and what you want is a war
but what you deserve is to be witnessed.

BERNARDINE "DINE" WATSON

WHERE IS THE LOVE?

Music is the place
where love goes
in the bluest times

Dancing a two-step
love and music
always together

Life is a blues song
laugh cry feel
sing the harmony.

AMANDA CHU

CONNOR, THE NATIONAL GUARD IS WATCHING

you teach me to cartwheel in Lafayette Square. I'm too scared
to kick my legs high enough, but you don't say anything about it.

We race in winter coats like children. You show me places
in the city I had never heard of: the Big Chair, the Go-Go cafe.

We joke that the city is so nice without the people. At a diner,
we take turns shooting my scrunchie back and forth like a gun.

We exchange details about future plans, lovers. Nearby, someone
argues about war. It is my turn next, and I don't know what to say:

How do I tell you that before this I didn't want to get out of bed?
I know I'm supposed to be hopeful, but it's hard to be interested.

I see you find your aim, your finger is pointed at my chest.
You say something I can't remember now. I brace for it.

TARA CAMPBELL

LOST AND FOUND

We lost our space. We weren't the ones who moved, though. We didn't shift position. The space slid out from underneath us while we were preoccupied with our jobs, our kids, our aging parents, our aching backs, our faltering sight, our heartburn clawing its way up our throats. We didn't move, but still we slipped, while tap-dancing for our supper, eyes locked on everything we had to keep up in the air, our hands a blur, faces tight from grinning. And still, we lost our space. No one cared what we thought anymore, no one featured us on their deep dives into the psyche of the country, let alone its basic needs. But did we mind? Sure. At least, at first. Initially we minded very much. Until we let that first demand drop. Did the world end? No. We just felt a bit more at ease. So we let a second obligation drop, then a third. The tap dance slowed to a soft shoe, then we finally said fuck it and just sat down. It felt good, catching our breath, letting all those responsibilities bounce around us. We picked up the few that really mattered and had a little game of toss, just between us, something we could sustain. We let all those other shoulds and musts roll around, curious to see if they would lift themselves up. Some did. In fact, most did. Turns out we were all right, floating in our whole new space, finding ourselves again.

MIHO KINNAS AND E. ETHELBERT MILLER

THE COLORS OF LOVE

James Baldwin is thinking
about writing a novel.

His characters want to move
to another country and give each
other different names.

Beauford Delaney tells Baldwin
he should use more color
in his sentences.

Desires and regrets
reflect the many shades
of skin color in hallway
light.

The blues are known
to turn shadows a darker
hue before midnight.

Charcoal gray reminds
Baldwin of Harlem and the warm
tinted touch of a brother's love.

ABBIE MULVIHILL

DIGITAL DC

The past came screaming through my door
in psychedelic technicolor today.
My white teeth and eyes floating
in an electrically charged hot bar of neon shots
from thirty years ago. Our loss is my gain.
He perfectly captured the repetition and
mind-jumping inebriation of our Capitol youth.
No wonder I called him the bad man.
I love who we were in our flirtatious, drunken
twenties. Innocent of innocence. Senate softball
sprats enjoying our freedom, while
committing glorious capital offenses.

KIM ROBERTS MEIKLE

MY PROPOSITION

I'm sending an overture to your skin,
an appeal to the musky sweetness
that lingers on your shirts like witchcraft.

I'll answer your summons, respond
to your nocturnal invitations.
I'll write a proposal, bid on your contract,

follow your guidelines' farthest compass.
I'm a caravel in your great armada.
The night is so wide and restless,

it pulls you out on its insistent tide.
Where you lead, wherever you lead,
I'll petition you for more of you,

lean hard into your heat,
put a motion on your table, second it,
and ask only to keep on asking.

MARIO MELO

FRIED YUCA

My hippocampus chews on smells—
linoleum throwing me back, toward
my grandmother's house. The greasy
pots and worn through pans

(in familiar condition) touch my nostrils
as mothers and aunties, well,
they teach me gospel.

Other children shriek, "it's lunch time!"
as mosquitos reach
for their different sized nets.

CHRISTINA TUDOR

RIPE

Grandma teaches you how to make eggplant parm, how to be a woman, how to slip the knife inside and break the purple skin into even rounds using the tip of your thumb, how to put in a tampon, how to remove the copper stains from your day-of-the-week underwear, and how to sweat out the eggplant with salt because it helps remove the bitterness, and Grandma holds a seed out to you on the tip of her finger, says *that means it's a female eggplant*, and don't forget, *you've got to be careful now that you can have a baby* and *boys will take advantage of a nice girl like you*, knife in her hand, in the air, crushing garlic under her cracked palms, and she tells you to whisk two eggs, and together you'll coat the eggplant in yolk with one hand and blanket with breadcrumbs, oregano, and parmesan with the other then layer—eggplant, marinara, mozzarella— then bake until the cheese spills over the edges like a wave, and later, after you've become a woman, after boys have taken advantage of a nice girl like you, after you've followed grandma's rules because no baby grows inside of you but nothing else takes root either, and after grandma falls asleep and doesn't wake up, bake eggplant parm again, again, again, and when seeds stick to your palms, swallow one, hope it'll grow into something else.

SUSAN BUCCI MOCKLER

THE BIRDS OF MCINTOSH LAKE

One of my favorite t-shirts reads *enough*
in lowercase white bubbly letters on a black
background—a memento from one of many
recent marches on Washington protesting gun
violence, insurrection, inequality. This morning,
I notice I'm wearing the shirt, unintentionally,
on a walk around beautiful McIntosh Lake.
A Great Blue Heron stalks its prey, diving
with measured precision. A *congregation*
of snowy egrets gathers across the lake, virtually
resembling a snowfield. A pelican glides low
to the water on its monstrous wings. What symphony
is this? What unexpected interlude? I cannot say,
but this morning, in this moment, I let it be enough.

ANDREW BERTAINA

A LOVE LETTER TO MICROPLASTICS

To the microplastics flowing through the river, through my veins, through the small vessels of my heart and into the deep recesses of my groin, to everything that has been discarded, thrown away, bought and then quickly forgotten, a love letter to all the plastic bags floating in the grocery store parking lots, even the one in *American Beauty*, to the plastic bottles floating down the sun-skittered river that ran through the municipal park of my childhood, to the six-ringed cans that we later learn choke sea birds, to the piles of it found in the belly of whales, to the floating islands of plastic, which we'll live on when the long experiment we've been running comes to an end, to the plastic gidgets and gadgets my children have brought home over years, which I've tossed into the plastic trash bag, thrown out into the plastic garbage bin, where it has been carted off down these winding streets like rivers of youth, so far away from me that I never thought I'd ever see them again, but like a lover, they have come back to me, those dear microplastics, who ford the rapids of my arteries, who trouble my insides, those plastics, like memories, which accompany me everywhere now, to the store, to Rome, to the bridge in Rock Creek Park frozen over this winter, to the cadence of own beating heart, which says, over and over again, like a prayer in my youth, ashes to ashes, microplastic to microplastic.

SEAN FELIX

ON SWANN STREET

in a gingko shower
of yellow leaves
we forgot that we were late.

we forgot that a price
was laid on our bodies—
on our time.

we forgot tear gas, flash bangs,
and cobalt mines.

we stopped history
with our kiss,
and our skin glowed gold.

ZACH POWERS

HERE OFTEN

I love a wrong feeling, and
they're all wrong, more or less.

Or it's the right feeling at the wrong
time in the wrong company. No,

there's no sin in making do nor
making out in the buzzy barlight.

But prickled up like that, grinny
and spinning, that's no time to ask,

Maybe *this*?

LAUREN D. WOODS

WHEN U.S. BOMBS HIT IRAN

It's 2025, you're watching *When Harry Met Sally*, and there you are back in 1989, when you were seven—the age of your youngest—and it's four months before the Berlin Wall falls, and America is a road trip with a friend, America is an airport where Harry runs into Sally, and then it's the promise of a long walk together over the years.

And halfway through, you and your husband go for a walk, when your phone buzzes, and your friend has texted *Holy fuck*, with a link to the headline "President Trump announces air strikes on nuclear sites in Iran." And then you stop and tell your husband and follow the text with *I'm speechless.*

But you're not, you talk about it with your husband, how we scuttled the deal, about friends who are leaving the country and the endless options that don't feel like options, because you have put down tender roots all over this city that you love.

And this is the movie's halfway point, where Harry has to reckon with his cynicism versus love, and you have to decide: Do you, or do you not, finish the movie tonight?

You worry about an enflamed world already populated by cynics. And although you know how the movie ends, it's important to see it out. Not because it matters, but because, for a little while, you are back to 1989, and though America is tarnished by a whole patchy history, we have always cared about love.

ROBERTA BEARY

AFTER MAKING LOVE IN OUR WATERGATE CO-OP WITH RIVER VIEW

My husband wipes off my pink lipstick. Then gets to work on my blush and eyeshadow. Drops the soiled handkerchief at my feet. I place it in Grandma Rosa's wicker basket. Can you believe he let me keep something from my old life? Right until I told him yes, life was divided into workdays (me late for the 8 a.m. bus, me reading *Pride and Prejudice* in the cafeteria, me calling 'see you tomorrow!' to my coworkers), and weekends (me running to ballet class Saturday afternoon, me slow-sipping cappuccino at the Italian market Sunday morning). Now I've moved from in-person to telework. So my husband can watch me on cameras he installed. Weekends are always the same: church and bible study. My pink ballet slippers sleep in a satin bag under the sink, behind the toilet tissue. One day I'll practice at the barre again. Hour after hour. But for now the towel rack in the powder room is perfect.

tea for one
the hairline crack fills
with honey

SALLY HUGGINS TONER

BICYCLE LOVE POEM

When we are young and pedal at sea level
blessed with those to hold the bases of
our seats over most uneven places—
We don't know the physics and the magic
that might happen with the letting go.
When we dizzy around in playground time,
When we try too hard with all and fall, climb
hills of adolescence, when we dress
our rides with gears, mechanizations, we
forget. It's pumping feet and bleeding knees
and sweat it takes to fly. Today, let's pry
the dust from our seats and play. My love, let's place
our cards in spokes of bicycle wheels, feeling
rumbles through our summers breaking fall.

KARA OAKLEAF

SHARED WALLS

Yes, it's sometimes a radio in the apartment below blaring Metallica at 4:30 a.m., or a neighbor and six of his friends shouting at a football game, their voices thundering a chorus of *motherfuckers* while you're babysitting your niece. Sometimes arguments late at night from the wall behind your headboard, where another couple lies awake in bed, and you want to pound the wall but do not because you can hear they are so tired, too. Sometimes it's stepping out of these concealed worlds onto small balconies, and a man whose name you do not know hands you a beer across the open space, and the little boy you hear jumping off the furniture all day has carefully lined up a row of painted rocks on the railing. Sometimes it's the smell of some spice from an unrecognizable dish overpowering the air flowing into your kitchen, you suddenly hungry for something you can't name, and sometimes it's a mother and a baby and a lullaby sung on the other side of the wall, the lyrics foreign, but you recognizing it anyway, because the rhythm of all lullabies, in all languages, is so close to breath. Sometimes that mother's voice is the thing that makes you think all of it, all the chaos coming through your walls, is music. Even the football guys, when the play goes right and their curses turn joyful and they hug so violently you hear their bodies crashing into each other. You love them just as hard.

MARY ANN LARKIN

A WISH

I wish I had a friend
who wasn't dead,
like Jill, with her golden hair
and slow ways,
who came over around ten—
after I'd taken the boys
to nursery school—
to be with me
in my tiny courtyard,
to sit and pull errant grass
from between unyielding bricks,
and talk, and talk
and talk forever,
until even time, at last
rolls over on its back
and is still.

CESAR FELIPE

ALL THIS HAS HAPPENED BEFORE

I cannot tell you what's already happened.

In confirmation: a thumb stroke of holy oil across your small brow, dipped twenty years ago in the tears that tipped out of my own father's eyes.

Of your ready hand raised to shield your eyes from the fluorescent light that would not be turned on until hours ago, warming you in the absence of skin and fluid and things in between.

The film already beat thin by the million could-have-beens who made way for you. Ignored by the myth you were the strongest, the fastest, the first to arrive.

And you could still be all of those things. Or anything else. The pride that I lean on in the bleachers. The link that I share just to see you reply. The pit that I fall in. But only just once—and they've happened before in my own tears as a child, shaking in your grandmother's arms because I am five years old and do not want to die. "That's a long way from now," she told me. Then she prayed, and though I do not pray anymore, will you lay a palm on my cheek? In my last breaths, will you be there, holding my hand? Saying this already happened, so don't be afraid. Love that exists in the waiting, before you were born. Before the Big Bang, which then had a new name: All This Has Happened Before.

DAVID EBENBACH

NOT A SONNET

We always forget not to kiss each other good night
on Yom Kippur. Yom Kippur is not for kissing—
not for kissing, or anything else that comforts: nice
shoes, or warm bread, or a glass of water at any
temperature, unless it's to look at and contemplate
the way G-d is refracted through the world like light
through that glass. That would be a good use for
Yom Kippur. But among other things love is a habit,
and as we settle into bed, just starting to be hungry
and thirsty, we forget for a moment what night it is,
and with a quick kiss assure one another that we are
here, the two of us, thank G-d. And then each realizes
and we touch our own lips. Tinily scandalized. Childlike.
Refractions.

KESHNI WASHINGTON

RE·FRAC·TION:

I was a nomad. The creature purring, pushing against my shin wasn't my cat. The kettle whistled, precursor to a warm teacup pressed into my hand, in a kitchen that was not mine. I went to work in daylight, but then rotated nights through friendly houses. It was dangerous at home. In that house lay ten years' worth of shattered life shards, shredding me with every breath. He didn't love me, that way, anymore. "I'm leaving." Those words were heavy objects hurled against our marriage. I broke, crumbling with the past which now seemed like lies and then evaporating with the future that would now never exist.

For six months, these women opened their spare rooms, couches, shared their tea and their cats with a nomad. On weekends they would sometimes even gather for group sleepovers. Sentinels between me and the dark. Food and laughter flowed. Then, the quiet confessions, no longer about crushes, now about marriages, careers, and our deepest insecurities within them. Still the light was gone out of me, no gravity of worth to keep it. Until my therapist asked me to put him aside, to examine why these sentinels were still here, doing all this, for me. I genuinely could not answer. In the following days, as I dwelled on this question, something shifted. As I gazed at myself through the beautiful brown eyes of these women, footholds formed in the vacuum within. My friends refracted my light back into me. This is real love.

MICHAEL CHANG

KISS OF LIFE

Everybody loves a winner, but when you lose it's just you and your bedroom—Tory Dent

let me try to write a poem that doesn't suck
i'm in a kathy acker novella
wheel that bitch to x-ray
she once called greeks 'freeloaders'
now kimberly guilfoyle is trump's ambassador to greece
'if she delivers, who cares if she's in a see-thru dress ?'
—is that quoted from maduro's reply brief ?
donald judd, u may approach
he's just screaming into the void
how's the reporting from beyond the wall ?
the worst will surely happen in 30 years
i'm a different kind of wife
i was the godfather of that style
hated by most gays
except the ones w/ class & taste
i secretly beg, waiting all afternoon for ur big bird
spit in my mouth like a proper daddy
transfixed by the light
couples w/ no money throwing back fireballs
sex toys, the oar goes deep
admiring this epochal poem
arnold's many aliases, scooby-doo's talent agent

i invited ur ex to tea
i scrutinize ur gf, applying strict scrutiny
'they did see my pushback abt the language'
—shut the fuck up abt ur emails
azn boy in puffer jacket, quiet now
dark eyes blinking
lobster trap
just sit there & watch ur anti-phishing videos
they fail u in that deep way
luca, stupid w/ confidence
heard nothing abt it
elliott abrams did not serve
mcgeorge bundy did not serve
john mccain did
what good it did
hard to believe
we accepted the disaster, this flotsam
maybe something u need to work on
forget the ones that got away, angry
church hats & BBQ
judged by touch
only the best will do

SAMANTHA J. POMERANTZ

WHEN ALL THE EVIDENCE POINTS TO THE END OF THE WORLD

This is all I can do: find a way
to keep my heart open.

Put my time into answering the phone, become
a scallop shell for another heart to pour into.

I can hold your grief and mine
while the cars rumble by. Outside the tires' revolutions

reverberate between the still houses, the bare oak
trees, the snow-crusted yards. Everywhere I look

there is life in progress, space in quiet attentiveness.
Even with all this wounding, I can choose

to live nested between my ribcage and breastbone,
safe in the steady beating: wearehere wearehere wearehome.

I can breathe into my community, paint pain into meaning,
give anger all the air it asks for, let the waves crash, and remember.

ZEINA AZZAM

WE PLANT TREES IN GENOCIDE

We bury our dead, yet we plant trees.

—Rev. Munther Isaac, Palestinian Christian Pastor in Bethlehem, West Bank, Palestine

The earth knows us. We trust soil, sun, rain.
On this same land, bombs land.
We bury our dead. We bury our trees.

Yet our children gather seeds.
They ask us to imagine oranges and pears.
We are summoned by the name of cactus fruit: صبر sabr, patience.

And fists will open, will plant.

Our ancestors, at peace in death: the roots, the love we know.
They are the earthworms, minerals, oxygen,
old branches and stones anchoring trees.

In our homeland we thirst for water and light.
We dream of farming, even in hunger.

Below, tears and breaths mingle, a helix in the soil.
Hopeful tendrils curl toward the sun.

MEG EDEN

LOVE TO

love to the guy at Panera shamelessly filling two half gallon containers of tea

love to my chiropractor, who explained if i'm autistic, isn't everyone to some degree?

love to the anonymous twitter user who retweets my workshop and says I'm underqualified to teach

love to the man who coughed in my face on the street

love to the anti-maskers

love to the man who flipped a table at our restaurant last night

love to the boy manspreading next to me on the plane

love to the child in the shopping cart who screams and screams and screams

love to the woman who cut in front of me in the TSA line, then climbed under the strap to cut off someone else

love to all of us who do desperate things in desperate circumstances

love to all of us who do ugly for no good reason

love to all of us with the love we wish to see

CAPITAL LOVE CONTRIBUTORS

Zeina Azzam, a Palestinian American writer, was the Poet Laureate of Alexandria, Virginia, for 2022-2025. Her publications include *Some Things Never Leave You*, *Bayna Bayna*, *In-Between*, and poems in literary journals and anthologies. She is the poetry editor for *We Are Not Numbers*, a writing program for youth in Gaza.

Roberta Beary (they/she), winner of the Bridport Poetry Prize, was born and raised in Jamaica Estates, New York and resides in Bethesda, Maryland. Their work appears in *Tiny Love Stories* (*Modern Love/New York Times*), *Rattle*, *HAD*, and other publications. *Crazy Bitches* (MacQ, 2025) is their fifth poetry collection.

Andrew Bertaina is the author of the essay collection, *The Body Is A Temporary Gathering Place* (Autofocus, 2024); the book-length essay, *Ethan Hawke & Me* (Barrelhouse, 2025); and the short-story collection, *One Person Away From You* (Moon City Press Award Winner, 2021).

Chris Biles (she/her) lives and works in Washington, DC. She enjoys playing with light and dark, losing herself in music, anything outside, and some words here and there. She is published in magazines, journals, and anthologies in print and online. www.marks-in-the-sand.com / Instagram: @marks.in.the.sand.

Brandon Blue is a black, queer poet, translator, and educator from the D(M)V. Their work appears in *Foglifter, Frozen Sea, &Change*, and more. Their work is also featured in the Capital Pride Poem-a-Day event. Their chapbook, *Snap.Shot* (Finishing Line Press, 2023), was named in Poetry Mutual's *Best Books of 2023*.

Emily Blumberg is a writer and producer living and working in the Capitol Hill neighborhood. Her writing is published in *The 51st, Teen Vogue, Autism Spectrum News*, and *The Michigan Daily*. She founded the Purple Line Collective, an arts and culture collective for young creatives in the DC area.

Caroline Bock is the author of four books including the novel *The Other Beautiful People* (Regal House Publishing, 2026). She is the co-president/prose editor at the Washington Writers' Publishing House.

Olivia Braley is a writer from the DMV. The author of the chapbook *Softening* (ELJ editions, 2021), Braley's work has appeared in *the Southern Humanities Review* and elsewhere. She is the co-founder of Stone of Madness Press and a member of the Discount Guillotine collective. Find her at oliviabraley.com.

Tara Campbell is a writer, teacher, and fiction co-editor at *Barrelhouse*. Publication credits include *Masters Review, Wigleaf, Electric Literature, Uncharted Magazine*, and *Strange Horizons*. She's the author of two novels, two hybrid collections, two short story collections, and a chapbook of sestinas. She lives in Seattle, Washington. www.taracampbell.com.

Alex Carrigan (he/him) is a Pushcart-nominated editor, poet, and critic from Alexandria, VA. He is the author of *Now Let's Get Brunch* (Querencia Press, 2023) and *May All Our Pain Be Champagne* (Alien Buddha Press, 2022).

Grace Cavalieri is celebrating 49 years on public radio, with "The Poet and the Poem" now from the Library of Congress. She holds AWP's "George Garret Award." Her latest books include *Fables From Italy and Beyond* (Asterism Books, 2025) and *The Third Eye*. She lives in Annapolis, MD.

Michael Chang (they/them) is the author of *Things a Bright Boy Can Do* (Coach House, 2025) and *Heroes* (Temz Review/845 Press, 2026). Their work has appeared in *AGNI, American Poetry Review, Greensboro Review, Harvard Review, Iowa Review*, and *POETRY*. A Virginia native, they live in Manhattan.

Kirsten Shu-ying Chen is the author of *light waves* (Terrapin Books, 2022). The recipient of a MacDowell Fellowship, her writing has been twice-nominated for a Pushcart Prize, shortlisted for The Autumn House Press Prize, and appears in *Adroit Journal, Verse Daily, The New York Times,* and elsewhere. www.kirstenshuyingchen.com.

Amanda Chu is a writer and journalist from Queens, New York. She lives in Washington, DC with her two cats.

Ellen Aronofsky Cole is the author of two poetry collections—*Notes from the Dry Country* (Mayapple Press, 2019) and *Prognosis* (Finishing Line Press, 2011). Journal publications include *Bellevue Literary Review, Gargoyle, Little Patuxent Review, Potomac Review, Innisfree, Beltway Poetry Quarterly, Fledgling Rag, New Verse News, Ekphrastic Review*, and *Mid-Atlantic Review*.

Jona Colson is a poet, educator, and translator, and the author of *Said Through Glass*. He is co-president and poetry editor at Washington Writers' Publishing House.

Kyle G. Dargan is the author of six poetry collections, an Associate Professor of literature and creative communications at American University, and the Books Head for Janelle Monae's creative company Wondaland. Dargan also, along with Shyree Mezick, operates as the creative consulting firm SKKS Creates. More at www.american-boi.com.

Christina Daub is a Pushcart Prize and Best of the Net-nominated poet who lives in Maryland. She cofounded and edited *The Plum Review*, a national poetry journal. She translates from Spanish and German, and taught poetry at George Washington University and The Writer's Center. www.christinadaub.com.

Barbara Westwood Diehl's poems and stories appear in a variety of journals, and her chapbook *Foolish* (L+S Press, 2025) was selected as the annual Mid-Atlantic Chapbook Series winner. She is senior editor of *The Baltimore Review*.

Therese Doucet's historical novel with magical realist elements, *The Prisoner of the Castle of Enlightenment*, was published by D.X. Varos in February 2020. She is a former Fulbright Fellow and Fellow of the Virginia Center for Creative Arts. She lives in the Cathedral Heights neighborhood of Washington, DC.

David Ebenbach is the author of eleven books of poetry, fiction, and non-fiction. David lives with his family in Washington, DC. He teaches creative writing, literature, and creativity, and supports teaching practices of faculty and graduate students at Georgetown University. You can find out more at www.davidebenbach.com.

Meg Eden is a Maryland author of the 2021 Towson Prize for Literature-winning poetry collection *Drowning in the Floating World* (Press 53, 2020) and *obsolete hill* (Fernwood Press, 2026) and children's novels, including the Schneider Family Book Award Honor-winning *Good Different* (Scholastic, 2023). Find her online at megedenbooks.com.

Cesar Felipe is a data scientist who tries to write. More at cesarfelipe.substack.com.

Sean Felix is a citizen poet from Washington, DC. He has performed and read with local jazz bands and literary reading series. He has published poems with *Broken Spine, Humana Obscura, the Mid-Atlantic Review, Sunday Mornings at the River*, and numerous other literary journals.

Jason Gebhardt is the author of the chapbook *Good Housekeeping* and the full-length poetry collection *Dictionary of Air* (Washington Writers' Publishing House, 2027). He is the recipient of multiple Artist Fellowships from the DC Commission on the Arts and Humanities.

Sid Gold's fifth collection of poetry is *Very Eyes* (Poets' Choice, 2023). He is a two-time recipient of the MSAC Individual Artist Award for Poetry and was named one of Baltimore Magazine's Best Poets. His poems have appeared in reviews and journals for more than forty years. He lives in Hyattsville, MD.

Holly Karapetkova is Poet Laureate Emerita of Arlington, Virginia, and recipient of an Academy of American Poets Laureate Fellowship for her work with young poets. Her third book of poems is *Dear Empire* (Gunpowder Press, 2025).

Miho Kinnas and **E. Ethelbert Miller** began writing Twoness Poems in 2021, a term they coined, in which they take turns writing line by line. Miho is a poet and translator living in South Carolina. Ethelbert is an award-winning writer, literary activist, and broadcaster living in Washington DC.

Mary Ann Larkin, author of *That Deep and Steady Hum* (Broadkill River Press, 2010) and *The Coil of the Skin* (Washington Writers' Publishing House, 1982), is the co-founder of Big Mama Poetry Troupe and Pond Road Press. Larkin is an alum of Yaddo and the Jentel Foundation.

Chanlee Luu is a Vietnamese-Chinese American writer from Southern Virginia. She is the winner of the 2024 Jean Feldman Poetry Award from the Washington Writers' Publishing House, which published her debut collection, *The Machine Autocorrects Code to I.*

Josh Mahler lives and writes in Virginia. His poems have appeared in *Denver Quarterly, Tar River Poetry, Quarter After Eight, South Carolina Review, Kestrel, The Louisville Review, Valparaiso Poetry Review, Potomac Review, The Southern Poetry Anthology*, and elsewhere.

Kim Roberts Meikle is the author of seven books of poems, most recently *Q&A for the End of the World*, a collaboration with Michael Gushue (WordTech Editions, 2025). Meikle co-curates DC Pride Poem-a-Day and co-directs the Pride Poetry Fellowship at the Arts Club of Washington.

Mario Melo is an Angolan poet living in Washington, DC, whose work has previously been published in *Lovestruck Inkwell*. Mario holds a Master's in English & Literary Studies from the University of Denver. They are a substitute teacher, freelance writer, and participant in DC's poetry open mic circuit.

Susan Bucci Mockler is the author of the poetry collection *Covenant (With)* (Kelsay Books, 2022), and her poetry has appeared in a number of literary journals, including *the Mid-Atlantic Review, peachvelvet, Maximum Tilt*, and several anthologies. She teaches at Howard University in Washington, DC and lives in Arlington, Virginia.

Abbie Mulvihill, a retired US federal government employee, lives in Silver Spring, MD. Abbie began publishing her poetry in 2022. Her poems appear in *The Best American Poetry* blog's "Pick of the Week," *Innisfree Poetry Journal, Anacapa Review, Beltway Poetry Quarterly*, the anthology *North Coast Voices 2025*, and other publications.

Samantha Neugebauer is the author of the story collection *Villains* (Washington Writers' Publishing House, 2027) and craft book *Teaching Writing through Story Reimaginings: Adaptation as Critical Practice* (Bloomsbury, 2028). She lectures at NYU in Washington, DC, serves as senior editor of *Painted Bride Quarterly*, and holds an MFA from the Writing Seminars at Johns Hopkins.

Kaetochi Nwodo is a writer living in DC with her wife, cat, and long-suffering plants. In her free time, she enjoys cuddling with said wife and cat, eating ice cream, and watching horror movies. She is working on a speculative memoir about grief. You can find her on IG @kaetochiwrites.

Kara Oakleaf's stories appear in *New Flash Fiction Review*, *Smokelong Quarterly*, *matchbook*, and elsewhere, and have been selected for Best Small Fictions and the Wigleaf Top 50. She earned her MFA at George Mason, where she teaches and directs Watershed Lit and the Fall for the Book festival.

Keith David Parsons is from West Virginia, lives in DC, and is less conflicted about it than you might think. He believes a poem without a message is like a big hole without spikes at the bottom—why would you dig it? The AdMo Parsons Project / www.kristophanes.substack.com.

Samantha J. Pomerantz (she/her) is a writer and personal development coach. She earned a BA in creative writing from Elon University. She lives in Maryland.

Zach Powers is the author of the novel *The Migraine Diaries* (JackLeg, 2026), the novel *First Cosmic Velocity*, and the story collection *Gravity Changes*. He serves as Executive & Artistic Director for The Writer's Center and *Poet Lore*. Originally from Savannah, Georgia, he now lives in Arlington, Virginia. ZachPowers.com.

Alfonso "Sito" Sasieta is a poet, dancer and gatherer of peoples. He is the Outreach Coordinator for L'Arche Greater Washington, DC and a principal dancer for the acclaimed Cuban dance company, DC Casineros. His poems and prose can be found in *Image, Sojourners, The Michigan Review,* and elsewhere.

Susan Scheid lives in Washington, DC, and is the author of *True Blue* (Finishing Line Press, 2025). Susan has received several Artist Fellowships from the DC Commission on the Arts and Humanities. Read more at: www.susanscheid.com.

Tamar Shapiro's debut novel, *Restitution*, was published in 2025. Her writing has also appeared in *Poets and Writers, Electric Literature, Literary Hub*, and *The Washington Independent Review of Books*. A former non-profit leader, Shapiro received an MFA from Randolph College in January 2026. She lives in Washington, DC.

S. Shaw is the author of *The House of Men: poems*. His work has appeared in *African American Review, Split This Rock, Rhino, Rattle Literary Journal, Obsidian*, and elsewhere. He is a Cave Canem Poetry Fellow and a Pushcart Prize-nominated poet. He lives and works in Baltimore.

Laura Shovan's work appears in publications for children and adults. Her books include *Mountain, Log, Salt,* and *Stone* (Harriss Poetry Prize, Citylit Press, 2010) and *A Place at the Table* (written with Saadia Faruqi, Clarion Books, 2020). She lives in Maryland and teaches for Vermont College of Fine Arts.

Victoria Sosa is a writer, editor, and performing poet with a BA in English Writing from Loyola University New Orleans. A 2026 WWPH Fellow, she also writes for DC Theater Arts. Her work has been recognized by *Kinsman Quarterly*, the Del Shores Foundation, and the Tennessee Williams Literary Festival. Find her @morning.starlet.

Sally Huggins Toner (she/her) lives in Reston, Virginia with her husband and is an empty nester with two grown daughters. She is the author of *Anansi and Friends* (Finishing Line Press, 2019) and has lived in the Washington DC area for over 30 years.

Christina Tudor is a writer living in Washington, DC. Her fiction has been featured in *SmokeLong Quarterly, matchbook, HAD, Flash Frog, The Citron Review, Best Small Fictions*, and more. Her debut chapbook will be published by Thirty West in Fall 2026. www.christinatudor.com / @christinaltudor on social media.

Charlotte Van Schaack is a queer poet residing in Washington, DC. Their work often explores the relationship between identity, memory, and landscape. Their work has been published in *WWPH Writes, Screen Door Review, Dialogist*, and *Door Is A Jar*. @cvanschaack.writes on Instagram.

Keshni N. Washington's stories are influenced by two continents. Born and raised in an apartheid segregated township in South Africa, after more than a decade in the DMV, she has finally gotten used to Orion being the right way up in the night's sky. She writes to light signal fires.

Bernardine "Dine" Watson is a nonfiction writer and poet who lives in Washington, DC. Dine's book *Transplant: A Memoir* (Washington Writers' Publishing House Nonfiction Award Winner, 2023) was selected for National Public Radio's "Books We Love" and included in *Poets and Writers Magazine* "5 Over 50 Debut Authors" feature.

Maura Way attended Murch, Deal, Wilson, Mary Washington, and Boise State. She is the author of *Another Bungalow* (Press 53, 2017) and *Mummery* (Press 53, 2023). Maura has been a school teacher for decades, recently at a Quaker high school in Greensboro, North Carolina. Washington, DC is still home.

Tamia Williams holds a BA in English and Communications from Washington College. Her work, which spans various genres that capture her curiosity, aims to challenge, explore, and heal. She has been published by *great weather for MEDIA* and nominated for the *2020 Best Small Fictions Anthology*.

Lauren D. Woods is the author of *The Great Grown-Up Game of Make-Believe* (Autumn House Fiction Prize, 2024), which was longlisted for the PEN/Bingham Prize for Debut Short Story Collections. She lives in Washington, DC with her husband and fellow writer Andrew Bertaina.

The Washington Writers' Publishing House would like to thank:

DC Commission on the Arts & Humanities

Maryland State Arts Council

Jean and John Feldman, and all the individual donors and volunteers who help make our literary work possible.

Washington Writers' Publishing House is a 501c3 nonprofit cooperative. More information on supporting our mission to publish and celebrate the rich mosaic of writers from DC, Maryland, and Virginia at www.washingtonwriters.org

WASHINGTON WRITERS' PUBLISHING HOUSE

Writers from DC, Maryland, and Virginia... readers across the nation

Washington Writers' Publishing House is a nonprofit, cooperative literary organization that has published over 100 volumes of poetry since 1975, as well as fiction and literary nonfiction. The press sponsors annual competitions for writers living in DC, Maryland, and Virginia, and the winners of each category (poetry, fiction, and literary nonfiction or translation in alternate years) comprise our winter slate. In 2021, WWPH launched an online literary journal, *WWPH WRITES*, to expand our mission to further the creative work of writers in our region. In 2024, WWPH launched its biennial Works in Translation series. In 2025, to celebrate the press's 50th anniversary, WWPH published a landmark anthology, *America's Future: poetry & prose in response to tomorrow.* The press is also committed to an ongoing series of pocket-sized anthologies, including in 2026 *Capital Love.* More about the Washington Writers' Publishing House is at www.washingtonwriters.org.

www.ingramcontent.com/pod-product-compliance
Lightning Source LLC
LaVergne TN
LVHW051017080826
845145LV00009B/2667

* 9 7 8 1 9 4 1 5 5 1 5 4 7 *